Green with Red Spots Horrible

JEN McVEITY

Illustrated by
Leigh Hobbs

sundance™

Published by
Sundance Publishing
33 Boston Post Road West
Suite 440
Marlborough, MA 01752
800-343-8204
www.sundancepub.com

Copyright © text Jen McVeity
Copyright © illustrations Leigh Hobbs
Project commissioned and managed by
Lorraine Bambrough-Kelly, The Writer's Style
Designed by Cath Lindsey/design rescue

First published 1997 by
Addison Wesley Longman Australia Pty Limited
95 Coventry Street
South Melbourne 3205 Australia
Exclusive United States Distribution: Sundance Publishing

ISBN 978-0-7608-1937-1

Printed by Nordica International Ltd.
Manufactured in Guangzhou, China
May, 2012
Nordica Job#: CA21200579
Sundance/Newbridge PO#: 226970

Contents

Chapter 1
Act Normal

"Will you look at that boat!" said Dad.

"You're turning green again," warned Mom.

"I'm not," said Dad. He sat up quickly and checked his arms and chest. All he could see was suntan lotion and sand. But then he saw his legs. Bright green against the white sand — and getting greener.

"Act normal," said Mom. She spread a towel over Dad's legs and looked quickly around to see if anyone on the beach had noticed.

"You look like a goblin," said Samantha loudly. "A great green goblin."

Dad turned even darker green, and a large patch of purple started on top of his head.

"Quiet, Samantha!" ordered Mom. Now Mom's face and ears were turning red— bright red. She looked like a beet with eyes.

There were huge red stripes on her arms, too.

"What did I say?" asked Samantha. Her voice carried to about three groups of people lying nearby. They looked over, saw Dad's feet and Mom's face, and started to nudge each other and stare.

Samantha turned to my brother Rory. His face was turning red, too. Even his hair was changing color. "Are you sunburned or something?" she asked. "You look really red."

Rory's hands opened and shut a couple of times and suddenly went black. "Shut up, Samantha," he said.

She looked at me. I felt my own face start to prickle.

"All I said was . . ." Samantha's voice was loud.

"Shut up!" Rory and I yelled. "Just shut up!"

Chapter 2

Green with Envy, Blue with Cold

No one was quite sure how Samantha came to be staying with us.

"Aunt Tilly asked us to invite her," Mom said.

"Who's Aunt Tilly?" I asked. We'd never heard of her. But then we'd never heard of half of Mom's relatives. Her family was big.

"My mother's sister," replied Mom. "Or maybe she's a cousin." She frowned, trying to remember. "Anyway, she called and asked if Samantha could stay for a few days."

"It's been more like a few weeks," I said.

"Feels more like months," added Rory.

"Well, it can't hurt for a short time," said Mom.

She was wrong. Very wrong. Samantha had been in the house for only four days when my favorite CD, my secret hoard of chocolate, *and* two of my best books disappeared. Rory and I never played cards now. Samantha cheated like crazy and then cried if we didn't let her win.

She pulled the rope tight and tripped you at jump rope and called all our friends idiots to their faces. And if you left your lunch unguarded for more than three minutes, she stole everything — sandwiches, fruit, nuts, sometimes even the paper bag as well.

Then there was the problem of the colors. At first Dad thought it must have been the water that made us turn such strange colors.

The kitchen counter was covered with all these water filters he'd bought. He even filtered the bath water and the water we used to brush our teeth.

"It can't be the water," Rory said. "Otherwise everyone else on the street would be turning weird colors."

"Maybe it's something we're eating," said Mom. "All these preservatives and food dyes. It can't be natural."

Mom spent hours reading labels on food packages. We ate things called wheat germ and tofu and soy milk. And the only fruit we had was apples with the skin cut off. Nothing worked.

Ever watched a great basketball game and turned bright pink with excitement? Really hot pink?

Ever seen a brother miss his serve in tennis three times in a row — and turn a kind of blue-green-gray in frustration?

And Rory and I haven't watched a horror movie since the time we turned white all over at a really scary part.

Yet, Samantha never seemed to feel anything. She certainly never changed color. She just watched us and smiled a small secret smile nearly all the time.

Rory and I knew it was Samantha ever since that day in the supermarket.
We were always in the supermarket.
Samantha ate three times as much as anyone else in the house, including Dad.
On that day someone had turned up the air conditioning way too high.

"Brr, it's cold in here," said Samantha.

Mom nodded. "It sure is." She didn't notice her fingernails slowly turning blue. Then her hands. Then her arms.

"Er . . . Mom," I pointed.

Mom looked down. The blue was spreading to her shoulders and across her face. She looked weird.

"You're turning blue with cold," said Rory.

"How odd!" said Samantha loudly. She looked pink and normal as usual — and smug. "You do look strange!"

Everyone in the supermarket was starting to gather around, pretending they wanted milk so they could see the blue lady with her kids.

"Let's get out of here," said Rory. His face was turning a strange color, too, like mashed strawberries. You could see it spread like a wave over his neck and arms.

"You're really red," laughed Samantha.

"That's enough," said Mom. She put a blue arm on Rory's bright red one and pushed the cart into the checkout line. "We'll do the rest of the shopping later."

"Red with embarrassment," said Samantha really loudly. Rory turned even redder.

"Stop it," I ordered.

"Stop what?" asked Samantha. As if she didn't know!

I could feel the skin on my neck start to prickle. Samantha was watching me carefully.

"Are you all right?" she asked sweetly. "You look angry about something. A little purple around the edges."

"I'm fine," I replied. The prickling was spreading. I took a deep breath, dragged my eyes from hers, and thought of calm seas and lakes and tiny trickling streams.

TRICKLING STREAM
— MINERAL WATER —

The prickling slowly faded.

"Next, please," called the checkout woman. Samantha turned to smile at her. I didn't waste any time. I slid into another line and pretended to belong to a family with three screaming kids and a cart full of junk food.

Mom finally figured it out. After all, Rory and I had told her about twenty-seven times.

"She waits until you feel angry or sad or something," I said. "Then somehow she turns how you feel into a color."

"You know, purple for anger," Rory said. "Red with embarrassment, green with envy."

"Nonsense," said Mom, but she looked uneasy.

"How come Samantha never changes color?" I asked.

"How come she hardly ever laughs or cries or gets angry herself?" questioned Rory. "She doesn't seem to feel anything. No emotion. Hardly ever."

"All she ever does is smile to herself," I said. "She's watching us all the time. Like we're on TV or something."

Mom shivered. "You're being silly. Samantha is a perfectly normal girl. She walks, she talks, plays games and eats, just like you and me." She stopped talking and suddenly became quiet.

"Come to think of it," said Dad, "she does eat a lot."

"She never stops eating," I said.

Mom got even quieter. "You know," she said slowly, "yesterday afternoon Samantha ate the cooked chicken I was planning for our dinner. The whole chicken, bones and all," she added.

"I think we should have a talk with Samantha." Dad looked worried.

"It won't do any good," Rory said. "She always acts sweet and innocent and pretends it isn't her fault."

Mom sighed. "She is strange . . ."

"Send her home," I suggested. It was what we were all thinking.

"I agree. I think we should call Tilly," said Dad. "Right now."

Mom sighed and then slowly nodded. "You're right," she said, and reached for the phone.

That was when we found out there was no Aunt Tilly. No cousin even. No one in the family had heard of Tilly. Or Samantha.

Chapter 3
Puce for Putrid, Aqua for Awful

The colors got worse. Samantha got worse.

"You're looking tired," she would say to Mom. "A little gray around the edges." And Mom would turn a horrible washed-out gray, and her worried frown would deepen.

"Look at that car," she said to Dad, and watched his skin turn green. "All that power. Great colors. Wouldn't you just love that?"

She hid my homework, picked fights with our friends, and crashed every computer game we had until I thought I would stay purple and angry forever.

And she picked on Rory all the time. She would creep up behind him and whisper the colors into his ear so that Rory turned white or red or yellow and stayed that way for hours.

"You look kind of sick. All hot and flushed and red," she said. "You're not afraid of that huge dog, are you? But you sure look a little yellow."

An hour before his big tennis match, she tried to make him turn pink and gray stripes.

"You must be so excited," she said. "I can see you're pink with excitement. But you must be nervous, too. So nervous. Really, I'd be gray with nerves if I were you."

"Cut it out, Samantha," I yelled.

"Cut out what?" Samantha did her innocent act again.

"Turning our skin into colors!"

"I'd be careful if I were you," said Samantha. "You're turning all purple."

"Stop it!"

"I'm not touching you," she said.

"Just wait! I'll get you back. One day. One day!"

"You're turning green, too." That smug little smile hovered around her lips and stayed and stayed and stayed.

I was purple and green for a whole day
after that and had to miss going swimming
and rollerblading with the gang. It didn't
help that I kept wishing I could turn
Samantha's skin into colors, too. I had
a few good ones for her. Puce for putrid.
Green for ghastly. Aqua for awful . . .

We had to get rid of Samantha.

Chapter 4
Think Pink

"We can't just throw her out in the street," said Mom.

We were in Mom and Dad's bedroom having a secret conference while Samantha sat in the den watching a horror movie on TV.

"Why not?" demanded Rory. He'd felt carsick going shopping that morning, and Samantha had turned him yellow and green all over his face and chest. The colors were only just fading now. Parts of his ears were still bright red from embarrassment.

"Can't we tell someone?" said Dad. "Like one of those science groups or something."

"Great idea," I said. "And quickly."

"Will they believe us?" asked Mom.
"I mean . . ." Her voice trailed away.

She had a point. How did you explain to a stranger that a kid was turning you into a sickly-colored rainbow every day of the week?

"There has to be someone who knows about her," said Dad. "Someone who would believe us."

Dad stayed late at the office and spent hours calling people from different scientific groups, who asked a few questions and then hung up. Most days he came home gray-blue with frustration.

Mom turned more and more gray with worry and started buying food in bulk and serving Samantha's food on two huge plates. In every spare minute, Mom called her family and talked to cousins, more cousins, second cousins twice removed. Not one of them knew of Samantha.

Samantha's smug smile and the colors haunted our dreams and our days. It looked like we would be stuck with her forever.

"KAPOW!" yelled Rory. "ZAP! SINGGG!"

"RAAAP! KAPOW!" I cried. "Take that you space freak!"

We were in the very far corner of our backyard playing alien invaders.
We played it a lot lately.

"I'm playing, too." It was Samantha. Somehow she always found us.

"No way," said Rory. "You always ruin everything."

"I want to play," Samantha said. She didn't even bother to raise her voice. "I'm going to play."

"Drop dead," I said. "You're a real pain." I was so sick of her.

"You're mean!" she said. "Mean. Mean. Mean."

Suddenly Samantha stopped. She smiled her smug smile and looked straight at me.

"You're really, really orange mean," she said.

I tried to make my mind go blank. I tried not to think of orange. It was no use. I felt waves of bright, ghastly orange riding all over my body.

"Turn her back, you horrible little pest," ordered Rory.

"*You're* horrible," Samantha said. She took a big breath and smiled, "Green with red spots horrible."

"Think pink, Rory!" I cried. "Think normal!" The green spread, the red dots grew redder. He looked really bad.

"You're a brat," Rory yelled at her. "A snotty-nosed brat! A pink with black stripes brat!" He stopped and waited. Nothing happened, of course. Nothing at all.

"You're a white-faced, red-nosed pig," I tried, too. Still nothing.

Samantha grinned her mean grin again.

"You can't do it!" she cried. "No one from here can! Eat slime and suffer! You're a sickly pink- and green-striped kid."

I felt green spreading, running in great stripes down my legs. Bright pink was filling up the spaces in between. I started to sweat. I felt sick.

"Back off," Rory yelled.

"No way!" she cried. "You purple-headed, green-legged, red-eared brat."

"Stop that this instant!" It was Mom's voice. She must have heard. "Everyone get in here at once. Dinner's ready."

Dinner. Thank heavens. Food was the one thing that would get Samantha to back off. Rory and I almost ran for the back door.

"What happened?" Mom cried. I didn't even want to look at myself. Rory in green and red spots and purple was bad enough.

Samantha just marched right past her. "What's for dinner?" she asked. "I'm starving."

Well, when wasn't she?

Chapter 5
Going, Going, …Gone

Suddenly I looked at Rory. He looked at me. There was a tiny frown on his purple face, a half-smile on his red spotted mouth.

"I'm hungry, too," I said quickly.

"Me, too," said Rory.

"I bet you're *really* starving," I said to Samantha.

She was turning from Rory to me, looking puzzled. Mom was looking puzzled, too.

"You haven't eaten for hours," I said.

"Hours and hours." That was Rory. "You must feel really light-headed."

"And weak. Really weak. And tired," I said.

"You must be fading away with hunger."

"Fading away," I said.

Samantha was looking really puzzled now. Mom didn't say a word. She just sort of blinked and stared very hard at Samantha. I stared, too. Samantha was starting to look weird, like she was getting all blurry around the edges.

"What's happening?" Samantha had seen the expression on Mom's face.

"You really are fading!" whispered Mom.

"Fading away with hunger," said Rory. "You're so hungry . . ."

"So starving . . ."

Samantha was really pale now.

"I'm not!" she cried.

"You are. You're always hungry. You're weak with hunger." The color was draining right out of her now.

"Not ever enough to eat." Rory was almost whispering.

"Hungry . . ." I said. I could see the furniture on the other side of the room. Right through her head. "Starving . . ."

"Fading away . . ."

The colors on us were fading, too. Slipping away to normal.

"No!" cried Samantha. "No!" But even her words were faint. "Fading away . . ." It was really hard to see her now. My eyes ached from looking.

"Fading. Going now . . ."

"Going . . ."
"Going, going . . ."

As we watched, the last bit of color ran out, and she just sort of faded right out of sight.

"Gone."

We haven't seen her since.

About the Author

Jen McVeity

Jen was once a teacher and freelance journalist. She now specializes in writing for children, and has over a dozen chapter books and two teenage novels in print. Jen lives in Melbourne, Australia, with her husband and two children, who act as (very ruthless) story-testers.

Her writing uses lots of dialogue, and she likes to make people laugh. "You learn a lot about yourself and the world when you laugh," she says.

Jen has jumped off cliffs, skied glaciers, flown on a circus trapeze, and traveled around the world at least five times. She calls this research for her writing. Her family calls it having a good time.

Leigh Hobbs

Leigh Hobbs was born in the city of Melbourne, Australia, but grew up in a country town. At school he was never any good at sports or math or science, but he could always draw well. After studying at art school, his first job was at Luna Park in Sydney, where he supervised the repainting of a merry-go-round, and built two huge funny sculptures that are now in a museum in Sydney.

Leigh draws and paints all of the time. *Old Tom* is his best-known comic creation.